Bring on the Funny!

A Collection of SpongeBob Jokes

Stephen Hillenburg

Based on the TV series *SpongeBob SquarePants*® created by Stephen Hillenburg as seen on Nickelodeon®

SIMON SPOTLIGHT
An imprint of Simon & Schuster Children's Publishing Division
1230 Avenue of the Americas, New York, New York 10020
Jokes from the Krusty Krab copyright © 2005 Viacom International Inc. All rights reserved.
Nautical Nonsense and *Classroom Crack-ups!* copyright © 2006 Viacom International Inc.
All rights reserved. *For Singing Out Loud!* copyright © 2008 Viacom International Inc. All rights
reserved. NICKELODEON, *SpongeBob SquarePants*, and all related titles, logos, and characters
are registered trademarks of Viacom International Inc. Created by Stephen Hillenburg.
All rights reserved, including the right of reproduction in whole or in part in any form.
SIMON SPOTLIGHT and colophon are registered trademarks of Simon & Schuster, Inc.
For information about special discounts for bulk purchases, please contact Simon &
Schuster Special Sales at 1-866-506-1949 or business@simonandschuster.com.
Manufactured in the United States of America 1109 OFF
First Edition 1 2 3 4 5 6 7 8 9 10
ISBN 978-1-4424-0187-7
These titles were previously published individually by Simon Spotlight.

Bring on the Funny!

A Collection of SpongeBob Jokes

Simon Spotlight/Nickelodeon
New York   London   Toronto   Sydney

CONTENTS

Jokes from the Krusty Krab

by David Lewman

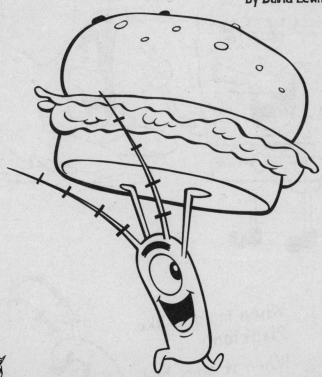

Simon Spotlight/Nickelodeon
New York London Toronto Sydney

SpongeBob: What does food start out as?

Sandy: Baby food.

SpongeBob: What kind of food do you feed to sharks with your bare hands?

Squidward: Finger food.

When is food like Plankton?

When it goes bad.

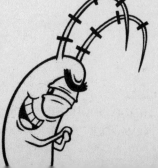

SpongeBob: Why do fishermen like to fish where there are tons of mosquitoes?

Sandy: 'Cause they get lots of bites!

SpongeBob: Why should you never eat in a dirty house?

Squidward: Because you'll bite the dust.

What do you get when you eat a frozen Krabby Patty?

Frostbite.

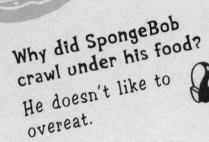

Why did SpongeBob crawl under his food?

He doesn't like to overeat.

Why did Patrick refuse to crawl under the table?

He didn't want to be underfed.

What did SpongeBob say to the Krabby Patty?

"Pleased to eat you!"

What did the Krabby Patties say when they saw their friend in Patrick's hands?

"What's eating him?"

SpongeBob: What do you call a huge lizard that only eats in the evening?

Patrick: A dinnersaur.

Squidward: Did the spatula decide to catch the patty or drop it?

SpongeBob: It left it up in the air.

SpongeBob: Why did the customer step on his check?

Squidward: He wanted to foot the bill.

Squidward: Knock-knock.
Customer: Who's there?
Squidward: Men.
Customer: Men who?
Squidward: Menu, or are you ready to order?

Mr. Krabs: What's the difference between a wiener and someone who grabs all the spots?

SpongeBob: One's a hotdog and the other's a dot hog.

Mrs. Puff: Which fruit is the saddest?

SpongeBob: The blueberry.

Sandy: What did you lose at the Chum Bucket?

SpongeBob: My appetite.

SpongeBob: How did Patrick get food all over the mirror?

Squidward: He was trying to feed his face.

Patrick: What happened when the patty met the bun?

SpongeBob: It was lunch at first sight.

SpongeBob: What do you get when you cross a gull and a swallow?

Sandy: A sea gulp.

Patrick: Which part of the ocean is the thirstiest?

SpongeBob: The Gulp of Mexico.

SpongeBob: Knock-knock.
Customer: Who's there?
SpongeBob: Goblet.
Customer: Goblet who?
SpongeBob: Gobble it down—it's a Krabby Patty!

How did the Krabby Patty feel when Squidward left him on the grill too long?

It really burned him up.

Why did Patrick sign up for percussion lessons?

Mr. Krabs told him to drum up new business.

JELLYFISH JAM

Is it hard to guess Patrick's favorite dessert?

No, it's a piece of cake.

Why did SpongeBob eat the Mystery Patty from the top down?

He wanted to get to the bottom of it.

Mr. Krabs: What did the restaurant owner say when the fisherman brought him free fish?

Squidward: "What's the catch?"

What's the difference between a mini-Krabby Patty and the sound a duck with a cold makes?

One's a quick snack and the other's a sick quack.

SpongeBob: Why did the frozen boy patty throw himself at the frozen girl patty?

Sandy: He wanted to break the ice.

Mr. Krabs: Why did you paint squares on the customer?

Patrick: Uh, because he said, "Check, please."

Why did SpongeBob throw paint during his fry cook's exam?

He wanted to pass with flying colors.

Patrick: Why can't boiling pots be spies?
SpongeBob: They always blow their covers.

Why did SpongeBob jump over the eating area?

Mr. Krabs told him to clear the table.

SpongeBob: Why did the soup refuse to leave the pot?

Sandy: It was chicken.

Mr. Krabs: Why do stand-up comics love to have eggs in their audiences?

SpongeBob: It's easy to make them crack up.

Why did Patrick bring a shovel to the Krusty Krab?

SpongeBob told him to dig in.

SpongeBob: How did the water feel after it washed the dishes?

Squidward: Drained.

What happened after Squidward said he'd never, ever eat alphabet soup?

He ate his words.

Patrick: How did the pancake's comedy act go over?

SpongeBob: It fell flat.

Patrick: How did that leave the pancake?

SpongeBob: Flat broke.

Why does Patrick fill his house with bread in the winter?

So it'll be nice and toasty.

Why did SpongeBob train a mouse to clean the Krusty Krab?

He wanted it to be squeaky clean.

Patrick: Why don't patties sleep on the grill?
SpongeBob: Because they'd spend the whole night tossing and burning.

Why did SpongeBob think the grill was angry?

It flared up at him.

Pearl: Why didn't the ketchup tell the mustard how he felt about her?

SpongeBob: His feelings were all bottled up.

Mr. Krabs: How did the ice cream react to leaving the freezer?

Squidward: It had a total meltdown.

SpongeBob: How did the napkin do in the poker game?

Squidward: It folded.

SpongeBob: What do you get when you cross a bird with a chili?

Squidward: A woodpepper.

Why did SpongeBob tie
a rope to the seat and
lift it to the ceiling?
Mr. Krabs told him to
pull up a chair.

Pearl: Why was the
pepper exhausted?
Mrs. Puff: Because it
had been put through
the mill.

Why did Mr. Krabs put all his money in the freezer?

Because he wanted cold cash.

Why was the patty grouchy?

It got up on the wrong side of the bread.

Patrick: How did the milkshake feel about his time in the blender?

SpongeBob: He had mixed feelings about it.

What's Plankton's favorite kind of bread?

Shortbread.

Sandy: When does butter do its best?

SpongeBob: When it's on a roll.

What did Patrick say to the customer when he filled in for Squidward?

"May I taste your order?"

Mr. Krabs: How did the onion feel about being sliced?

SpongeBob: It really got under his skin.

SpongeBob: When does food make you itch?

Patrick: When you make it from scratch.

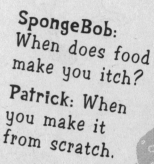

How does SpongeBob say good-bye to the patties when he leaves work?

"Spatulater!"

Why did SpongeBob toss a sandwich at Sandy on her birthday?

He wanted to throw her a surprise patty.

Why did SpongeBob put a circle of Krusty Krab sandwiches around his house?

He wanted to have an outdoor patty-o.

What do they call a stall in the Krusty Krab restroom?

A Krabby Potty.

SpongeBob: Knock-knock.
Customer: Who's there?
SpongeBob: Stan.
Customer: Stan who?
SpongeBob: Stan in line to order, please.

SpongeBob: Knock-knock.
Squidward: Who's there?
SpongeBob: Betty.
Squidward: Betty who?
SpongeBob: Bet he orders
another Krabby Patty.

Patrick: Knock-knock.
Squidward: Who's there?
Patrick: Al.
Squidward: Al who?
Patrick: Al have a double
   Krabby Patty with cheese.

Mr. Krabs: Knock-knock.
SpongeBob: Who's there?
Mr. Krabs: Donna.
SpongeBob: Donna who?
Mr. Krabs: Don a uniform before you start work.

Patrick: Which big, mean fish bakes the best bread?

SpongeBob: The Great Wheat Shark.

Why did SpongeBob jump up on the stove? He wanted to play King of the Grill.

How would SpongeBob like working in a ship's kitchen?

It'd be right up his galley.

SpongeBob: What do you call a tortilla filled with ice?

Sandy: A *brrr*-ito.

SpongeBob: What do chickens eat when they wake up?

Sandy: Peckfast.

Why did Patrick attach four tires and a steering wheel to the table?

Because Mr. Krabs told him to bus it.

Mr. Krabs: What kind of cup is impossible to drink from?

Squidward: A hiccup.

Sandy: Why did the piece of corn try to join the army?

Squidward: Because he was already a kernel.

Patrick: What do ghosts order with their Krabby Patties?

SpongeBob: French frights

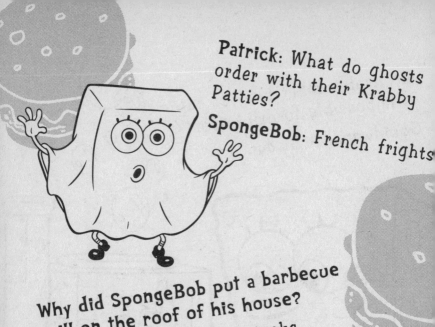

Why did SpongeBob put a barbecue grill on the roof of his house?

He wanted to raise the steaks.

Sandy: Where do vegetables go to kiss?

SpongeBob: The mushroom.

Why did Patrick throw the T-bone in a blender?

He wanted to make a chocolate milksteak.

SpongeBob: What do ducks eat for lunch?

Patrick: Quackaroni and cheese.

Sandy: What's green and comes on a bun?

Plankton: A hambooger.

Sandy: What comes in a tortilla and tells excellent time?

Squidward: A tick-tocko.

SpongeBob: If corn could talk, what kind of voice would it have?

Mr. Krabs: Husky.

SpongeBob: What would it say?

Mr. Krabs: "Shucks, I'm all ears."

SpongeBob: What did the waiter say to the frog?

Squidward: "You want flies with that?"

What did SpongeBob say when he ran out of cabbage? "That's the last slaw."

I'm full!

THE END

NAUTICAL NONSENSE

A SPONGEBOB JOKE BOOK

BY WENDY WAX

Simon Spotlight/Nickelodeon
New York London Toronto Sydney

Why were SpongeBob's suspenders sent to jail?
For holding up his SquarePants.

What goes "Ha, ha, ha, plop!"?
SpongeBob laughing his head off.

What happened when SpongeBob sat on the chewing gum?
He became SpongeBob ChairPants.

Who is the snootiest sponge in Bikini Bottom?
SpongeSnob.

Why does SpongeBob prefer saltwater?
Because pepperwater makes him sneeze.

Where does SpongeBob point his sneeze?
Atchoo!

What did SpongeBob say to the Flying Dutchman?
How do you boo?

Who didn't clean his pineapple?
SpongeSlob.

SpongeBob: What doesn't get any wetter no matter how hard it rains?
Patrick: The ocean.

Why did Patrick bring a chocolate bar to his dentist appointment?
He wanted a chocolate filling.

Why does Patrick prefer to swim at night?
He's a starfish.

Why did the bubble gum cross the road?
Because it was stuck to SpongeBob's shoe.

What was wrong
with Patrick's
pencil story?
It didn't have a point.

Why did Patrick walk as
he played the guitar?
He wanted to get away
from the noise.

What is the Flying Dutchman's favorite kind of party?

A come-as-you-were party.

Why did Squidward play his clarinet while standing on a chair?

So he could reach the high notes.

Why did Squidward keep his clarinet in the fridge?
So he could make cool music.

How does Squidward spell "disaster"?
S-P-O-N-G-E-B-O-B.

Squidward: Ouch! I threw out my back again.
SpongeBob: Check the trash before it's picked up!

Customer: Waiter! This coffee tastes like sand!
SpongeBob: That's because it was only ground this morning.

Knock-knock.

Who's there?

Dewey.

Dewey who?

Dewey have to eat
Krabby Patties again?

What happened when the Flying
Dutchman lost his anchor?

He haunted for it.

Why do some people call Mr. Krabs a "doughnut"?
Because he loves money.

What is Mr. Krabs's favorite part of the football game?
The quarterback.

How does Mr. Krabs double his money?
By folding it in half.

How much does Mr. Krabs eat?
Just a pinch.

What are two things Mr. Krabs refuses to serve for lunch?

Breakfast and dinner.

What happened when the Flying Dutchman got a job at the Krusty Krab?

He became the Frying Dutchman.

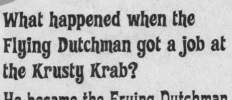

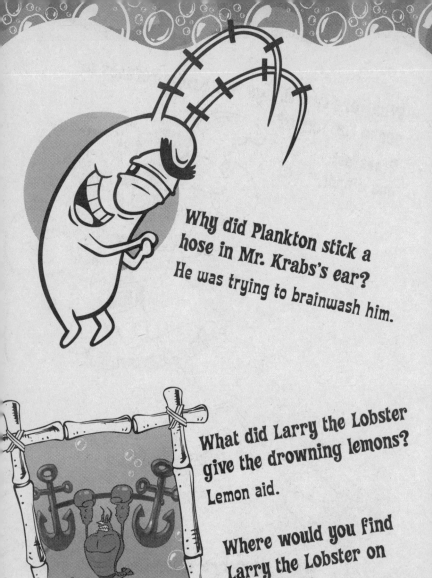

Why did Plankton stick a hose in Mr. Krabs's ear?
He was trying to brainwash him.

What did Larry the Lobster give the drowning lemons?
Lemon aid.

Where would you find Larry the Lobster on Halloween?
At the Boo Lagoon.

What does SpongeBob call Gary when he's riding in the passenger seat?

His carpet.

How did SpongeBob stop Gary from leaving slime in the backyard?
He put him in the front yard.

What did Pearl become on her trip to the Arctic?
A blue whale.

What musical did Mr. Krabs plan to take Pearl to see on her birthday?

Fiddler on the Reef.

NOW SHOWING...

Fiddler on the **Reef**

What did they do when the musical was sold out?

They saw a dive-in movie instead.

What did SpongeBob call Patrick
when he fell in the swamp?
Muddy buddy.

If Gary got in trouble, where would he go?
Snail jail.

How does Gary keep in touch with his family?

Snail mail.

Mrs. Puff: SpongeBob, have your eyes ever been checked?

SpongeBob: No, they've always been blue.

Sandy: What do you call milk that is too far away to see?
SpongeBob: Pasteurized.

Why did Mrs. Puff wear sunglasses to school?
She had bright students.

Who did Mermaidman become when he got lost in the Arctic Ocean?
Brrr-maidman.

How much did Patchy the Pirate have to pay to get his ears pierced?
A buck an ear.

Who wears an eye patch and is always itchy?
Scratchy the Pirate.

How did SpongeBob make a jellyfishing net?
He sewed a bunch of holes together.

Patrick: What does a jellyfish have on its tummy?

SpongeBob: A jelly button.

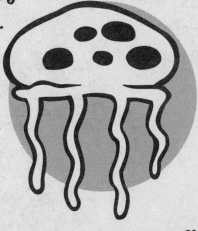

SpongeBob: What is the best way to catch a jellyfish?

Patrick: Have someone throw it to you.

Patrick: What buzzes, wobbles, and flies?

SpongeBob:
A jellycopter.

SpongeBob: What do you call a polar bear in Bikini Bottom?

Patrick: Lost.

Sandy: How does a boat show affection?

Patrick: It hugs the shore.

SpongeBob: What did one fish say to the other?

Squidward: If you keep your mouth closed, you won't get caught.

Books for Sale!

A Tourist's Guide to Bikini Bottom
by N. Joy Yerstay

Surfing Down Sand Mountain
by Howell I. Ever-Dewitt

The Krusty Krab Diet
by Watson Thimenue

Getting Rid of Plankton
by X. Terman Aite

Caring for a Pet Snail
by Walket Wunsaday

Sandy the Speedy Squirrel
by Sherwood Lyke Tewkatcher

How to Stop Procrastinating
by Alex Playne Layder

SpongeBob's Secret to Life
by M. Brace Itt

Mrs. Puff: What's the capitol of Bikini Bottom?

SpongeBob: The letter B.

SpongeBob: What do you call two pieces of seaweed that get married?

Sandy: Newlyweeds.

32

Mrs. Puff: What gallops through Bikini Bottom?

Patrick: A seahorse.

Knock-knock.
Who's there?
Doug.
Doug who?
Doug a hole in the sand.

What would you get if you cloned
SpongeBob five hundred times?
A SpongeMob!

Why didn't the judge believe the Flying Dutchman?
Because he could see right through him.

Who haunts underneath
SpongeBob's bed?
The Flying Dustman.

What is easy for SpongeBob and Patrick to get into but hard for them to get out of?

Trouble.

How did SpongeBob make a bandstand?

He took away their chairs.

How did SpongeBob get straight As
in Mrs. Puff's class?

He used a ruler.

What kind of steps did SpongeBob take when
Squidward chased him out of the Krusty Krab?

Great big ones.

Why did Patrick install a knocker on his rock?
He wanted to win the No-Bell Prize.

When does the Flying Dutchman usually appear? Just before someone screams.

Why was it windy at SpongeBob and Patrick's bubble-blowing show?
Because of all their fans.

Why did Patrick put a strawberry under his pillow?
He wanted to have sweet dreams.

Where in Bikini Bottom did Squidward see an annoyed cashier?

In the mirror.

Squidward: Where do fish go when they don't feel well?

SpongeBob: To a sturgeon.

SpongeBob: What do you call a fish with no eyes?

Patrick: A fsh.

Patrick: Do fish ever have holidays?

SpongeBob: No, they're always in schools.

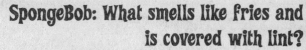

SpongeBob: What smells like fries and is covered with lint?

Squidward:

The Dusty Krab.

SpongeBob: What lives at the bottom of the sea and carries a lot of fish?

Mrs. Puff: An octobus.

Where is Patchy the Pirate's treasure chest?

Under his treasure shirt.

Mr. Krabs: Why did the fish tell excuses?

SpongeBob: To get off the hook.

What do you get when you cross Dracula with Patchy the Pirate?

A vampirate.

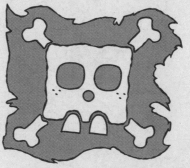

Why didn't SpongeBob do well on his report card?

Because his grades were below C-level.

How does SpongeBob know the sea is friendly?

It waves.

What game do Patrick and SpongeBob like to play?

Name That Tuna.

Mr. Krabs: Why did the fries run out of the restaurant?

Patrick: They were fast food.

What did SpongeBob break by saying its name? Silence.

Who is Squidward's favorite writer?
William Sharkspeare.

Why doesn't Plankton serve doughnuts?
He doesn't like the idea of the hole business.

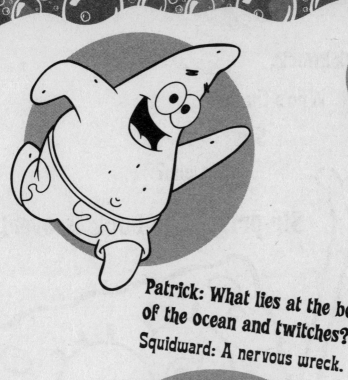

Patrick: What lies at the bottom of the ocean and twitches?

Squidward: A nervous wreck.

Knock-knock.

Who's there?

Sir.

Sir who?

Sir-prise! The book is over!

by David Lewman

Simon Spotlight/Nickelodeon
New York London Toronto Sydney

Why did Mrs. Puff become a teacher?

She's a classy lady.

Where did Sandy go before kindergarten?

Tree school.

Where did Squidward go before kindergarten?

Pre-scowl.

Mrs. Puff: Why did the cow study all night?

Sandy: She wanted to go to the head of the grass.

Squidward: What did the drinking fountain say to the student?

SpongeBob: "Have a nice spray."

How does SpongeBob get to the second floor of the school? He takes the square way.

What's big and lives in the water and works great on blackboards?
The Chalk Ness Monster

Sandy: Why did Patrick punch the library?
SpongeBob: His teacher told him to hit the books.

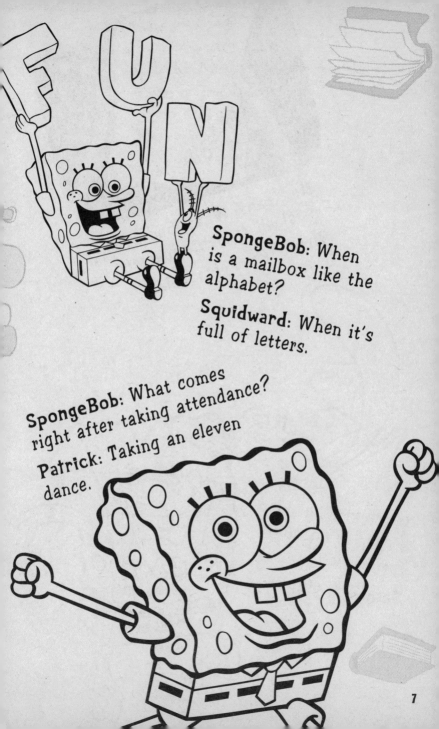

SpongeBob: When is a mailbox like the alphabet?

Squidward: When it's full of letters.

SpongeBob: What comes right after taking attendance?

Patrick: Taking an eleven dance.

You were right Spongebob! Those jokes are funny! Come on over to the Freedome tomorrow and celebrate. ♡ Sandy

Mr. Krabs: What kind of ship must all students master?

Mrs. Puff: Penmanship.

Patrick: What kind of pen is not good for writing?

Sandy: A pigpen.

SpongeBob: Why are skeletons so good at math?

The Flying Dutchman: They really bone up on it.

Why did the student take lipstick and eye shadow to school?

He had to take a makeup test.

SpongeBob: What's the best kind of pen when you're lost in the desert?

Sandy: A fountain pen.

Why did Patrick hit the test
with a tennis racquet?

He wanted to ace the exam.

What did Mr. Krabs
say when he found
an ancient bug in the
dictionary?

"Why, that's the
oldest tick in the
book."

SpongeBob: Why wouldn't the teacher show his students how to connect two points?

Pearl: That's where he drew the line.

Did SpongeBob complete writing the letter _i_ on time?

Yes, he finished right on the dot.

Patrick: Knock-knock.
Squidward: Who's there?
Patrick: Reese.
Squidward: Reese who?
Patrick: Recess is my favorite subject!

Patrick: Why was the soap always good in school?

SpongeBob: He never got in bubble.

Sandy: Where's the best place on a baseball field to take a test?

SpongeBob: Right field.

Mrs. Puff: What comes just before detention?

Patrick: C-tention.

What kind of test does Bubble Buddy hate the most?

Pop quizzes.

SpongeBob: Which part of the beach is the smartest?

Pearl: The quicksand.

Sandy: Why did Patrick put his test in his piggy bank?

SpongeBob: He wanted to save it for a brainy day.

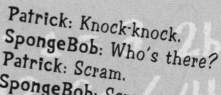

Patrick: Knock-knock.
SpongeBob: Who's there?
Patrick: Scram.
SpongeBob: Scram who?
Patrick: Let's cram for the big test tomorrow.

Why didn't SpongeBob study hard for his driver's license test?

He didn't want to start a traffic cram.

Patrick: Where do tests come from?

Mrs. Puff: The Exami-Nation.

Squidward: What makes you think Mrs. Puff finds you clever?

Patrick: She said I have a smart mouth.

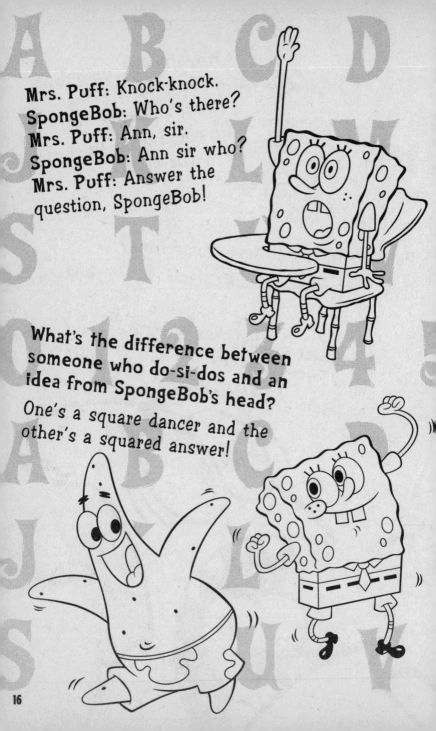

Mrs. Puff: Knock-knock.
SpongeBob: Who's there?
Mrs. Puff: Ann, sir.
SpongeBob: Ann sir who?
Mrs. Puff: Answer the question, SpongeBob!

What's the difference between someone who do-si-dos and an idea from SpongeBob's head?

One's a square dancer and the other's a squared answer!

What electronic gadget did Patrick buy just before the big test?

An answering machine.

Sandy: What kind of answer doesn't belong in school?

Mrs. Puff: A belly dancer!

SpongeBob: Why did the student write his math homework on his toes?

Sandy: He was trying to think on his feet.

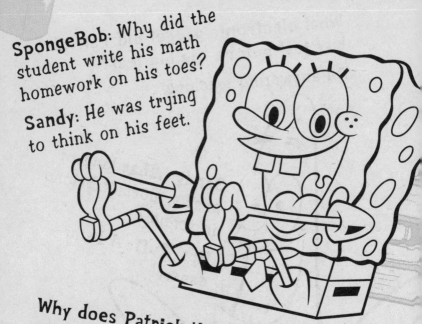

Why does Patrick think three, five, and seven are weird?

He heard they're odd numbers.

Why did Squidward sculpt a giant *A* out of clay?

He wanted to make the grade.

SpongeBob: What kind of test do they give in dancing school?

Squidward: True or waltz.

SpongeBob: What kind of test do they give in cooking school?

Mr. Krabs: Multiple cheese.

Sandy: What's the difference between a trunk full of gold and a quiz on yellow cheese?

SpongeBob: One's a treasure chest and the other's a cheddar test.

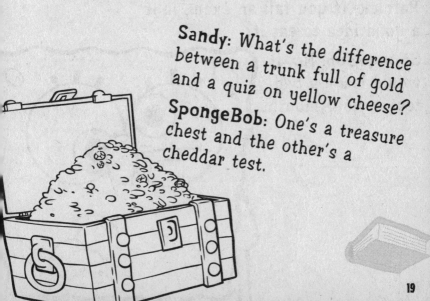

Why did SpongeBob bring a fly to school?

For shoo-and-tell.

Patrick: If you fail an exam, is it a good idea to eat it?

SpongeBob: No, it would leave a bad test in your mouth.

SpongeBob: Why do phones always sit in the front of the class?

Squidward: They love to be called on.

Sandy: How did the chicken improve her grades?

SpongeBob: She joined a study coop.

Why did Patrick bring slime to school?

For a goop project.

Why did Plankton bring a ladder to school?

He wanted to get high grades.

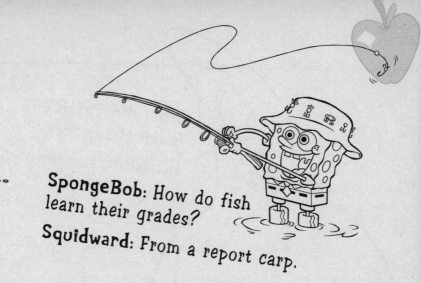

SpongeBob: How do fish learn their grades?

Squidward: From a report carp.

What book does Mr. Krabs hate to take out?

His checkbook.

What did Patrick
learn at school?

His ABZzzzzzzzz's.

What does SpongeBob write his homework
on when he's at the beach?

Sandpaper.

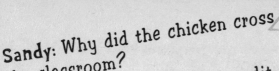

Sandy: Why did the chicken cross the classroom?

Mrs. Puff: To get eggs-tra credit.

Why did Patrick bring lots of pencils to gym class?

He wanted to end up with the most points.

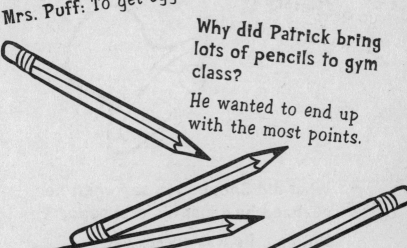

What book does Mr. Krabs love to study?

His bankbook.

Why did one school bell always go off before the others?

It was the ringleader.

What did SpongeBob say when he realized he'd lost his oral report?

Nothing. He was speechless.

SpongeBob: Which fish is best in English class?

Mrs. Puff: The grammarhead shark.

Why did SpongeBob's best friend take an apple to Mrs. Puff?

He wanted to be teacher's Pat.

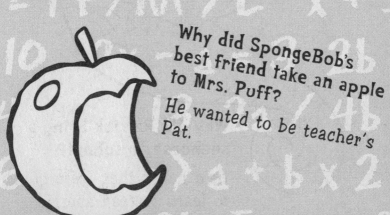

Why did Patrick build an extra room onto his rock?

His teacher told him to work on his addition.

Why did Patrick bring a seahorse to school?

He'd heard they were going to learn to read and ride.

What's the difference between a good student and Mr. Krabs?

One knows how to read and the other's known for his greed.

Why did SpongeBob call his math homework a "mystery"?

It just didn't add up.

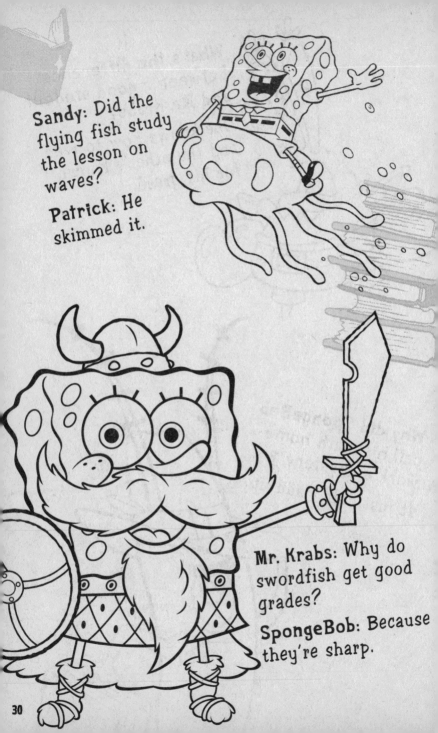

Sandy: Did the flying fish study the lesson on waves?

Patrick: He skimmed it.

Mr. Krabs: Why do swordfish get good grades?

SpongeBob: Because they're sharp.

What did SpongeBob think of
Mr. Krabs's lecture about pennies?

He couldn't make heads or tails
out of it.

When the teacher
asked him a question,
why did SpongeBob put
his hand in his mouth?

The answer was on the
tip of his tongue.

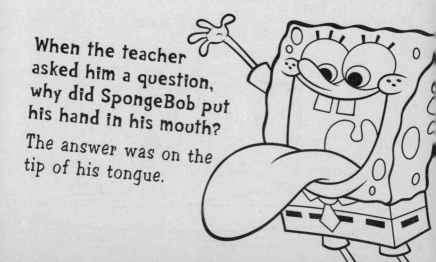

SpongeBob: How did the fish feel when school was cancelled?

Squidward: Like he was off the hook.

When does school turn Patrick's brain into a fish?

When it makes his head swim.

Why did Patrick lie down on the classroom floor?

The teacher told him to lower his voice.

How did Mr. Krabs get to know so much about the ocean?

He learned it from the Bikini Bottom up.

Why did SpongeBob climb up to the classroom ceiling?

The teacher told him to speak up.

Why did SpongeBob wrap sheets and blankets around his brain?

The teacher told him to make up his mind.

Squidward: Why don't cows get exact answers in math?

Sandy: They're always rounding up.

Why did Squidward spend hours talking about just one painting?

He wanted his students to get the picture.

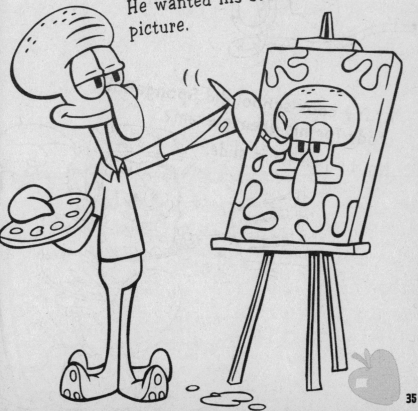

Did Patrick play jump rope at recess?

He decided to skip it.

At fry-cook school did SpongeBob study for his grease exam?

No, he just let it slide.

SpongeBob: Why don't astronauts make good students?

Sandy: They keep spacing out.

Why did Patrick bring frozen orange juice to class?

The teacher told him he needed to concentrate.

Why did Plankton steal his chair from school?

The teacher told him to take his seat.

SpongeBob: What did the ghost get on his exam?

The Flying Dutchman: A Boo minus.

Squidward: What's the worst kind of B to get on your homework?

Patrick: A bumblebee.

What's the difference between Patrick on a teeter-totter and Patrick looking at his report card?

The first seesaws and the second saw C's.

What did Patrick say when he saw the teacher marking his test?

"Go ahead, make my D!"

SpongeBob: When is a *D* not a bad grade?
Sandy: When it's a chickadee.

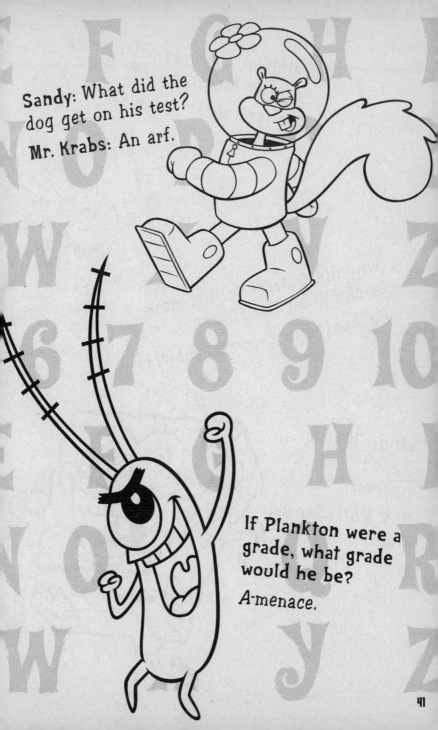

Sandy: What did the dog get on his test?

Mr. Krabs: An arf.

If Plankton were a grade, what grade would he be?

A-menace.

41

Patrick: Where do polar bears go after kindergarten?

SpongeBob: Frost grade.

Why did Patrick let his math book fall on the floor?

He wanted to drop the subject.

Sandy: Which grade is over the quickest?

Mrs. Puff: Second grade.

Where did Sandy go after second grade?

Furred grade.

Where do bacteria have P. E. class?

In the germnasium.

Which kind of musical note is
Mr. Krabs's favorite?

The quarter note.

Why did Patrick do
his math homework on
SpongeBob's back?

SpongeBob said Patrick
could always count on him.

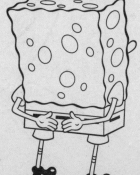

Why did Patrick hand in his test before he'd finished?

He ran out of guess.

Squidward: Was the school nurse willing to treat the sick sea monster?
Patrick: She said she'd give it a shot.

Why did SpongeBob do his school exercises over and over and over?

He wanted to be king of the drill.

What's Mr. Krabs's favorite kind of test?

Fill-in-the-bank.

SpongeBob: Why do pirates make bad students?

Mr. Krabs: Everything goes in one ahrrrr and out the other.

Patrick: Knock-knock.
SpongeBob: Who's there?
Patrick: Miss.
SpongeBob: Miss who?
Patrick: Mistakes are really easy to make.

Why can't Patrick divide by two?

He doesn't know the half of it.

SpongeBob: Is it hard to understand what "zero" means?

Patrick: Nah, there's nothing to it.

Patrick: Knock-knock.

SpongeBob: Who's there?

Patrick: Isabel.

SpongeBob: Isabel who?

Patrick: Is a bell ever going to end this school day?

FOR SINGING OUT LOUD!

SpongeBob's Book of Showstopping Jokes

by David Lewman

Simon Spotlight/Nickelodeon
New York   London   Toronto   Sydney

ROCK ON, SPONGEBOB!

- ★ **FAVORITE SONG:** "THE GARY IN THE SHELL"
- ★ **BEST MOVE:** TEARING MYSELF IN HALF
- ★ **WHAT I SHOUT AT THE END OF MY SONG:** "THANK YOU, BIKINI BOTTOM!"
- ★ **MOST EMBARRASSING TALENT SHOW MOMENT:** GOT THE MICROPHONE STUCK IN ONE OF MY HEAD HOLES

4

HOT TIPS

1. DO absorb a lot of water before you sing.

2. DON'T sing before you're READY!

3. DO make sure your shoes are shined and your tie is tied just right.

4. DON'T let Plankton trick you into singing the Krabby Patty recipe.

5. DO finish by floating away in a giant bubble.

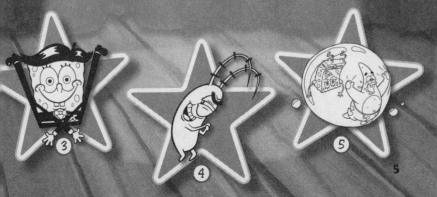

Patrick: How did the traffic light do in the talent contest?

SpongeBob: He stopped the show!

Why did Mrs. Puff bake bread for the talent show?

Because there's no business like dough business.

Why did Plankton enter the talent contest?

He wanted to steal the show.

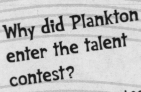

What do you call
a singing contest
for ghosts?

Scary-oke.

Patrick: Why did
the jellyfish enter
the talent show?

SpongeBob: He
thought it was a
stinging contest.

What's it called when
SpongeBob sings at
boating school?

A class act.

Patrick: What kind of furniture is best at talent shows?

SpongeBob: Musical chairs.

Does SpongeBob like dancing?

Yes, he gets a real kick out of it.

Sandy: Which tune is the sweetest?

Pearl: The caramel-ody.

What key is it best to sing in at the zoo?

Mon-key.

SpongeBob: What do you call a dancing rock?

Patrick: A stepping stone.

9

YOU'RE A STAR, PATRICK!

★ **FAVORITE SONG:** "ROCK-A-BYE, PATRICK"

★ **BEST MOVE:** THE BLANK STARE

★ **WHAT I SHOUT AT THE END OF MY SONG:**
"UH . . . I THINK I'M DONE."

★ **MOST EMBARRASSING TALENT SHOW MOMENT:**
REALIZED I WAS ONSTAGE

HOT TIPS

1. DO bring something to eat during your song.

2. DON'T mistake the microphone for a hot dog.

3. DON'T sing with your mouth full.

4. DO wear something over your underwear.

5. DO make sure your underwear is clean.

SpongeBob: Which singers are the cleanest?

Squidward: The soap-ranos.

Patrick: Who sings even higher than a tenor?

Plankton: An eleven-or.

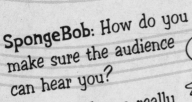

SpongeBob: How do you make sure the audience can hear you?

Patrick: Wear a really loud outfit.

Mrs. Puff: What kind of song do electric eels sing?

Mr. Krabs: Shock 'n' roll.

SpongeBob: What kind of song do parrots sing?

Painty the Pirate: Squawk 'n' roll.

What does Plankton sing into? A micro-microphone.

13

Why isn't Squidward friendly with his dance coach?

They started off on the wrong foot.

SpongeBob: Is it true that the dancers gave up?

Sandy: Yes, they threw in the twirl!

Sandy: What's the difference between a statue and an unsure singer?

SpongeBob: One's white marble and the other might warble.

Why did Plankton sweep up his footprints on the way to the talent show?

So he'd be a hard act to follow!

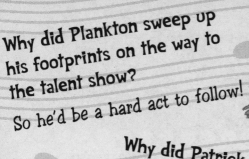

Why did Patrick bring a vegetable to the talent show?

He wanted to feel the beet.

Why did Patrick bring a baseball to the singing contest?

He'd heard it was important to stay on pitch.

TAKE IT AWAY, SQUIDWARD!

- ★ **FAVORITE SONG:** "I WANT TO HOLD YOUR HAND, HAND, HAND, HAND, HAND, HAND"
- ★ **BEST MOVE:** AWAY FROM SPONGEBOB
- ★ **WHAT I SHOUT AT THE END OF MY SONG:** "YOU PEOPLE WOULDN'T KNOW GOOD MUSIC IF IT STARED YOU IN THE FACE!"
- ★ **MOST EMBARRASSING TALENT SHOW MOMENT:** FOUND OUT THAT PEOPLE WOULD RATHER WATCH SPONGEBOB SWEEP THE STAGE

HOT TIPS

1. DO study classical music for years and years and years.

2. DON'T expect Bikini Bottom dwellers to appreciate it.

3. DO exactly as I do.

4. DON'T let SpongeBob talk you into practicing with him.

5. DO applaud loudly for me when I win.

Why did SpongeBob practice his arithmetic before the singing contest?

He'd heard you have to be really good at your addition.

Why did Sandy visit the Texas desert before the singing contest?

She'd heard that cactus makes perfect.

Why was SpongeBob scared to enter the singing contest?

He'd heard that first you have to make it through the dry-outs.

Why did Patrick sleep under his songs?

He'd heard they were sheet music.

Why did SpongeBob sprint over the top of the stage?

He wanted to be the runner-up.

SpongeBob: Who's second-in-command at singing contests?

Sandy: The voice president.

19

What kind of tuba does Patrick practice on every night?

A tuba toothpaste.

Squidward: Why do cymbals make bad drivers?

Mrs. Puff: They're always crashing!

Barnacleboy: Why was the reporter arrested at the music contest?

Mermaidman: He kept taking notes.

SpongeBob: Why aren't stingrays good singers?

Squidward: They're always flat.

Patrick: Why aren't swordfish good singers?

Sandy: They're always sharp.

Why did Patrick bring birthday paper to the singing contest?

He wanted to be a wrapper.

21

HOWDY, SANDY!

★ **FAVORITE SONG:** "GIT ALONG, LITTLE DOGFISH"

★ **BEST MOVE:** EXTREME MICROPHONE-STAND TWIRLING

★ **WHAT I SHOUT AT THE END OF MY SONG:** "THAT ONE'S FOR TEXAS!"

★ **MOST EMBARRASSING TALENT SHOW MOMENT:** ACCIDENTALLY LASSOED ONE OF THE JUDGES

HOT TIPS

1. DO warm up with a cowgirl yell: "YEE-HAH!"

2. DON'T forget to wear your air helmet if you're singing underwater (and you're a land critter).

3. DO remember to smile and show your big front teeth.

4. DON'T dare to sing a song about Texas unless you're FROM the great state of Texas.

5. DO work out before, after, and during your song.

What does SpongeBob sing to his Krabby Patties at bedtime?

A lullafry.

What's the name of SpongeBob's choir?

The Porous Chorus.

SpongeBob: What's huge, stomps around, and sings beautifully?

Sandy: Tyrannochorus rex.

Patrick: The judge said I sing like a baritone!

Squidward: No, he said he can't bear your tone.

Sandy: The judge said my voice was great!

Squidward: No, he said your voice was grating.

What is Plankton calling his new store for percussion instruments?

The Drum Bucket.

Patrick: Who brings you money when you lose your horn?

SpongeBob: The toot fairy.

Did Plankton meet the dance judge's standards?

No, he fell short.

Did SpongeBob enjoy playing the trumpet?

Yes, he had a blast.

How did Patrick get caught in a drum?

It was a snare drum.

Why did Patrick build a bonfire before the singing contest?

He'd heard it was important to warm up.

Patrick: How'd the firecracker do at the singing contest?

SpongeBob: Great—he burst into a pop song.

SING IT, EUGENE!

- ★ **FAVORITE SONG:** "I'VE GOT YOUR MONEY IN MY HANDS"
- ★ **BEST MOVE:** SPOTTING STRAY COINS ON THE STAGE
- ★ **WHAT I SHOUT AT THE END OF MY SONG:** "EAT AT THE KRUSTY KRAB!"
- ★ **MOST EMBARRASSING TALENT SHOW MOMENT:** MISTOOK JUDGE'S SHINY BUTTON FOR A QUARTER AND DOVE FOR IT

HOT TIPS

1. DO eat plenty of Krabby Patties before the contest.

2. DON'T expect to get free napkins.

3. DO tell all your friends to eat at the Krusty Krab.

4. DON'T ever eat at the Chum Bucket.

5. DO celebrate winning (or losing) with a big platter of delicious Krabby Patties.

How did SpongeBob's song go over at Mussel Beach?

He got a sandy ovation.

Pearl: Why was the student disappointed with the key the judge picked for him?

Mrs. Puff: He got an F.

Squidward: What do you call a group of nervous musicians?

Mr. Krabs: A sweatband.

Why did SpongeBob's boss take up the violin?

He wanted to be a fiddler crab.

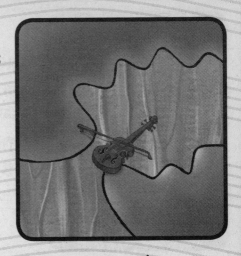

Sandy: What did the big wind tell the little wind before she sang?

SpongeBob: "Just remember to breeze."

Patrick: What kind of singing voice does corn have?

Plankton: Husky.

Why did Patrick climb up on the roof before he sang?

The judge told him to take it from the top.

Squidward: How did the mouse do in the singing contest?

Sandy: He squeaked through it.

SpongeBob: Why don't eggs sing high notes?

Mr. Krabs: They always crack.

Patrick: How did the pony do in the singing contest?

SpongeBob: He was a little hoarse.

Pearl: What musical instrument do geometry teachers like best?

Mrs. Puff: Triangles.

33

TELL IT LIKE IT IS, SHELDON!

- ★ **FAVORITE SONG:** "IF YOU'RE EVIL AND YOU KNOW IT, RAISE YOUR HAND"
- ★ **BEST MOVE:** RAISING BOTH ARMS AND LAUGHING MANIACALLY
- ★ **WHAT I SHOUT AT THE END OF MY SONG:** "BOW DOWN AND DO MY BIDDING!"
- ★ **MOST EMBARRASSING TALENT SHOW MOMENT:** COULDN'T REACH THE MICROPHONE

HOT TIPS

1. DO sing the Krabby Patty recipe if you know it.

2. DON'T expect to win if I'm competing.

3. DO build a remote-controlled robot to sing your song for you.

4. DON'T get in my way.

5. DO bribe the judges—but not with food from the Chum Bucket. (It doesn't work, believe me).

35

SpongeBob: How did the sledgehammer do in the contest?

Patrick: He was a smashing success.

Why did Patrick click his fingers through his whole song?

The judge told him to make it snappy.

Plankton: Why did the professional chef win the singing contest?

SpongeBob: He had a big range.

Pearl: Knock, knock.
Mrs. Puff: Who's there?
Pearl: Al.
Mrs. Puff: Al who?
Pearl: Altos over here, sopranos over there.

Why do chickens make good percussionists?

They're born with two drumsticks.

Patrick: Are high notes good?

Squidward: No, they're nothing but treble.

What's SpongeBob's favorite musical instrument?

The fry-olin.

Plankton: What kind of music always stinks?

SpongeBob: Reek 'n' roll.

Sandy: What kind of music is best for a ship at the bottom of the ocean?

Squidward: Wreck 'n' roll.

Mrs. Puff: What kind of music do rabbits like best?

Sandy: Hip-hop.

Squidward: What do you call a very short song sung by a cat?

Sandy: An itty-bitty kitty ditty.

HELLOOOO, MRS. PUFF!

- ★ **FAVORITE SONG:** "MY STUDENTS DRIVE UNDER THE OCEAN"
- ★ **BEST MOVE:** KEEPING TIME WITH A POINTER
- ★ **WHAT I SHOUT AT THE END OF MY SONG:** "NOW BACK TO CLASS!"
- ★ **MOST EMBARRASSING TALENT SHOW MOMENT:** I WAS SO NERVOUS I INFLATED IN THE MIDDLE OF MY SONG

HOT TIPS

1. DO study your lyrics carefully.

2. DON'T let SpongeBob drive you to the show.

3. DO wear a new hat.

4. DON'T ask Patrick to accompany you.

5. DO give your music teacher lots of presents.

SpongeBob: Why are fish such good musicians?

Mrs. Puff: They're always polishing their scales.

Sandy: How did the wrecking ball do in the singing contest?

Squidward: He brought the house down.

What happened to SpongeBob and Patrick's plans for dancing on a paper stage?

They fell through.

Squidward: How is a good dancer like a stairway?

Sandy: They're both full of steps.

Mr. Krabs: Why do math teachers always enter singing contests?

Mrs. Puff: They love to do their numbers.

Why didn't Patrick take the free guitar?

He heard there were strings attached.

SpongeBob: Do guitars get teased a lot?

Sandy: Yes, they're always getting picked on.

Patrick: What has wings and plays the guitar?

Mr. Krabs: The strummingbird.

Why did Squidward play a drum for the talent show judges?

They told him to beat it.

SpongeBob: Which musical instrument is the hardest to see?

Mr. Krabs: The foghorn.

SpongeBob: Which pet is the most musical?

Sandy: The trumpet.

Mermaidman: Why do violins make good presents?

Barnacleboy: They always come with a bow.

IT'S ALL ABOUT YOU, PEARL!

★ **FAVORITE SONG:** "HOW MUCH IS THAT OUTFIT IN THE WINDOW?"

★ **BEST MOVE:** THE POUT

★ **WHAT I SHOUT AT THE END OF MY SONG:** "SIT DOWN, DADDY!"

★ **MOST EMBARRASSING TALENT SHOW MOMENT:** DADDY JUMPED ONSTAGE AND SHOUTED, "THAT'S MY BABY!"

HOT TIPS

1. DO get all your friends to cheer for you.

2. DON'T let SpongeBob come up with your dance moves.

3. DO wear your hair in a ponytail.

4. DO throw an after-party.

5. DON'T throw it at the Krusty Krab.

Why did Patrick finish his song
by whacking a drum?

He wanted to go out with a bang!